'IF THE HOUSE IS TOO SMALL FOR YOU, I'LL MAKE IT BIGGER.'

YUKO TSUSHIMA
Born 1947, Tokyo, Japan
Died 2016, Tokyo, Japan

'The Watery Realm' ('*Suifu*') was first published in the May
1982 issue of the literary monthly *Bungei*. 'Of Dogs and
Walls' ('*Inu to hei ni tsuite*') was first published in the January
2014 issue of the literary monthly magazine *Shincho*. This is
the first time they have been translated into English.

TSUSHIMA IN PENGUIN MODERN CLASSICS
Territory of Light (forthcoming)
Child of Fortune (forthcoming)

YUKO TSUSHIMA

Of Dogs and Walls

Translated by Geraldine Harcourt

PENGUIN BOOKS

PENGUIN CLASSICS

UK | USA | Canada | Ireland | Australia
India | New Zealand | South Africa

Penguin Books is part of the Penguin Random House group
of companies whose addresses can be found at
global.penguinrandomhouse.com.

This selection first published 2018
004

'The Watery Realm'
Text copyright © Yuko Tsushima, 1982
Translation copyright © Geraldine Harcourt, 2018
'Of Dogs and Walls'
Text copyright © Yuko Tsushima, 2014
Translation copyright © Geraldine Harcourt, 2018

Set in 10.25 / 12.75 pt Dante MT Std
Typeset by Jouve (UK), Milton Keynes
Printed and bound in Great Britain by Clays Ltd, Elcograf S.p.A.

ISBN: 978–0–241–33978–7

www.greenpenguin.co.uk

MIX
Paper from
responsible sources
FSC® C018179

Penguin Random House is committed to a
sustainable future for our business, our readers
and our planet. This book is made from Forest
Stewardship Council® certified paper.

Contents

The Watery Realm

It was in the middle of the summer he turned five, as I recall, that my son discovered the Western-style castle in the window of the goldfish shop in our neighbourhood.

The castle was an aquarium accessory, designed so that when it was connected to an air pump the jet of bubbles raised the drawbridge. Though it would have fitted on the palm of my hand, each of its three turrets had a little window, and the whole thing was glazed a dark, purplish hue; small wonder my child wanted it the moment he set eyes on it. When it was submerged, what a mysterious beauty that quaint purple castle would surely reveal. Tiny fish would slip in and out of the turret windows, and if the drawbridge were lowered for them by turning off the bubbles, they would venture hesitantly inside through the entrance that this uncovered.

The price tag stopped me buying it for him on the spot. Besides, we didn't have a suitable aquarium, or an air pump, or any goldfish. All we had were five loaches he'd been given at nursery school, and those just sat in a corner of the apartment in a plastic container because we couldn't bring ourselves to throw them out.

The child, however, had his heart set on the castle. Deciding that if he couldn't turn to his mother he'd just have to buy it himself, he made the shop owner promise not to sell it to anybody else, because he'd be back. He was beginning to understand that money could buy you things. Already, he'd learned to gather up enough one- and five-yen coins to purchase a few ounces of sweets. He committed the castle's price to memory: two thousand three hundred yen. It might as well have been a million, or three hundred. It was all the same to him.

The shop sold several varieties of goldfish, plus killifish, green-shelled young turtles, newts, even crayfish. It also stocked aquariums in a range of shapes and sizes, along with accessories, water-care products and fish food. The easy-going man in his forties who served us seemed to be the owner of the little place. It was on our way down the hill to do the grocery shopping, and my son was in the habit of pausing outside every time we passed. But he had never wanted to have any of the creatures in the window. Now, the man, who sounded practised with children, answered his request, 'Sure. I'll leave it on that shelf there. So you go ahead and save up. You've a long way to go, but I'll be waiting.' I smiled at the man, as delighted as my son no doubt was. Resting his hand on the boy's shoulder, he flashed me a smile in return that said, Don't worry, it hasn't exactly been flying off the shelves.

My delight was simple. I was happy that my little boy had exchanged promises with this man, whose name we didn't even know. I was happy that the man had given him his whole attention. Though I guess all children were pretty much alike to him.

I was in such a good mood that I bought the loaches a hollow ceramic log and two artificial flowers – one yellow and one pink – which would bloom when placed in water.

As soon as we got home, I changed the loaches' water, filling the container almost to the brim, and added the log and the flowers. The log was fringed with plastic tufts of weed. Startled out of their usual torpor, the loaches writhed about in the new water. The artificial flowers unfurled, their petals gently swaying with each lurch. In water, their gaudy colours turned beautifully translucent, transforming the loaches' habitat into something almost enviable. The child was all excited, and so was I. We waited and waited, but the loaches showed no signs of going inside the log. Running out of patience, he said, 'I'll show them how,' and plunged his hands into the water to grab one.

'Give them time,' I said. 'They'll need to get used to the flowers first. But sooner or later they'll notice the tunnel themselves, and then they'll take to it.'

He nodded and was again lost in admiration of the flowers and the log in the water.

A few days later, the loaches entered the hollow log and stayed there. They took no interest in the artificial flowers, but then I don't suppose they would. The child gazed into the water every day. This wasn't enough, however. He hadn't forgotten the undersea castle. Whenever we went shopping, he checked at the store, made sure the castle was there on the shelf, and repeated its price to confirm it with me. Two thousand three hundred yen. Two thousand three hundred yen.

3

He started adding to his fund, one yen at a time. Four yen. Seven yen. Eleven yen. From time to time, he would report that the amount had grown and get me to count it. Told there were twenty-eight yen, he would ask, 'Is that more than two-thousand-three-hundred or less?' On hearing it was less, ever the optimist, he would ask, 'Am I nearly there?' and Mum would reluctantly nod. The child had yet to learn to count.

Autumn rolled on in this way, and then it was December. In his thoughts, the castle in the deep still glowed mysteriously. And around it was rapidly developing a whole underwater tableau. With the castle in the centre, artificial flowers bloomed in profusion while frogs and sea snakes and sharks frolicked among them. Each of these had its own house, and there was also a mountain, and on the mountain a ropeway. Meanwhile, the disobliging loaches had slipped our minds again.

How much had the child saved? Christmas was on the way. I told him I would make up the difference and he'd be able to buy the castle at last. I'd been looking forward to that day myself. The thought of our deal with the man in the shop always cheered me up. Be seeing you, I thought. I wanted to watch him nod approvingly when I told him, 'Look, we've kept our side of the promise.' Even if it was nothing much, it was a promise all the same.

We rushed off to the goldfish shop. At the sight of the child's face, the man said, 'Aha, so today's the day?' It was the response I was hoping for. 'Well done!' he went on. 'I knew you could do it. You've done such a great job, I'll give you a discount.'

For a while, we were both walking on air. We made our

way home blissfully. There we filled the aquarium which we had bought at the same time, connected the castle to the brand-new pump, and, holding our breaths, submerged it. If even my pulse was racing, it must have been quite a tense moment for the child. The beautiful underwater castle was about to make its long-awaited appearance.

But, being made of lightweight plastic, the castle wouldn't stay on the bottom. It bobbed right back up when I let go. It needed weighting. I tried inserting a corkscrew from the kitchen into the middle turret and, with that, it finally settled down. When I hooked up the tube from the pump and flicked the switch, bubbles spouted from under the drawbridge, which went up. But that was all. The airstream just burbled blandly towards the surface.

Now it was time to move the loach. Its fellows had died, one after the other, in the autumn or thereabouts. And as I hadn't been changing the water, which was now an opaque dark green, the last one might long since have been rotting on the bottom. I had become slacker than before about changing the water for fear of coming upon its corpse. Under the watchful eyes of my child – who was quite sure the loach was alive – I sluiced the water into the sink, scooping it out little by little. I removed the artificial flowers, green with gunk. The log shifted, and as it did I seemed to sense something stir in the water. It *was* alive. I felt suddenly afraid: what kind of living thing would be lurking in there?

I lifted the log out and then tried adding new water to the shallow remainder in the tank, diluting the murk. I threw that

5

water out as well. This time we found the loach, wriggling on the bottom. It appeared completely unchanged. I could only exclaim to the child, 'Wow, this one's a real survivor!'

'Mm,' he replied, unmoved. 'Go on, clean up the flowers, too.'

After rinsing the slime off the flowers and the log, I placed them in the new tank. Flowers to either side of the castle, log to the left. I put the loach in last of all. It dropped languidly through the water. On reaching the tank floor without sparing the castle or the flowers a passing glance, it started to nuzzle the glass, so I gave it some fish food. It pounced on that.

The child was staring steadily into the water. I stood beside him and stared at the tank myself. The effect was nothing like a deep-sea castle. Even the artificial flowers had lost their lustre. We needed a bigger aquarium, I grumbled to myself, though I was the one who'd picked a tank not much more than eight inches deep. Now, if I were to get a much bigger tank, and spread gravel on the bottom, furnish it with aquatic plants, set algae afloat on the surface and release gorgeously coloured tropical fish into the water, would the castle, too, finally come into its own and start to glow? Meanwhile, the child was gazing intently, wordlessly, at the underwater world. Perhaps a child could conjure up what he wanted to see from what was reflected on his retinas. Tranquil, dark, boundless depths. In their midst, a purple castle, lofty and cool. In place of winds, slow-moving currents. And all tinged with heatless, bluish light.

The Dragon Palace came to mind – the underwater castle

in the fable of Urashimataro. We mortals who dwell on land have always imagined, at the bottom of the sea, another world where we are not meant to go, chill and beautiful. The sea does seem a far more likely place of concealment than the sky, and, furthermore, water is a medium we know very well. An underworld. But in the Dragon Palace, unlike the Buddhist underworld, one encounters nothing unpleasant or frightening. Human emotions dissolve away as in a dream. The man in the fable who famously returned from the Dragon Palace discovered that time had had a different cadence down below. A hundred days had been a hundred years. Finding everything changed on land, he sighed, 'So, there was a catch.' Nothing he could do now would alter the fact that, as far as those long gone who had once depended on him knew, he had drowned one day, still in his prime. He had drowned, his kinfolk, too, had died off over the years, and that was the end of the story. Yet the man had returned from the watery realm, and on finding himself alone, he sighed, dreamily resigned to this having been the price; after all, he had been to the depths and returned. And what little he could remember of where he'd been had not felt at all bad. It was dark, and quiet. He had been in the water's intimate embrace. He was the water, and the water was him.

A major accident occurred at a coal mine. Some of the miners were rescued from deep below ground, but many others were given up for dead and water was pumped into the shafts to prevent further gas explosions. Many tons of it, until it filled the pit. The bodies were to be recovered after the water level receded in five or six months' time. Even now, those people lie in the water's deep embrace. A hundred days are a hundred years. Time passes silently; water is a seamless world. The water spreads through the earth, and the people in its embrace are now rivers, now the sea. Because we on terra firma sense the watery realm close by us, while knowing that it is out of our reach, we make it the bearer of some wish or hope – of feelings that might be called prayers. I do this, and so does my child. For we can never forget the watery realm, even though we haven't the remotest idea what it's like.

When I was a child, I was puzzled by the notion of 'underground water', as groundwater is called in Japanese. I pictured the ground on which I trod as a sheet over an expanse of water. That seemed awfully treacherous. If it was just floating there, then the ground might sink and the water show itself at any moment. I'd have to tread softly to avoid provoking the ground, and not even think about poking holes in it. For a time, I couldn't get these ideas out of my head. I wonder how old I was? I even avoided stepping in puddles, convinced I'd fall into the depths below like the girl in Andersen's fairy tale. When you looked down into them, they suggested entrances to an unfathomable world, or they did to me. Even today, watching my young child splash through puddles makes me uneasy.

The two places on the face of the earth that I knew best as a child were our house and the little graveyard next door. Among the plots there, I could actually feel the groundwater under the soles of my feet. Perhaps I'd got the idea that that water stretched away in every direction because I was too familiar, for a child, with a graveyard. Its enclosure lay just past our gate. A graveyard comes with narrow paths, and the earth in them was always moist. It was different from the earth in our garden, even though they were adjacent. I believed that if you removed a gravestone, you'd expose a hole down to the groundwater. I thought that was what a grave was. If you looked through the grave-hole, the sight of the groundwater and the drifting shoals of the dead would meet your eyes. That was why the stones mustn't be allowed to fall over or become dislodged. As long as the holes were covered, however, the graveyard seemed to me a good deal safer than other places, which were more porous; at least in the graveyard there wouldn't be random wild eruptions of the groundwater.

The first time I was taken to visit my father's grave, I must have been about three. As he had died two years before that, it would have been the second anniversary observance. But this is a surmise based on a photograph; I have no memory of the day. I visited my father's grave for the next special anniversary, too, four years later. On one of those visits, I don't remember which, the paths among the graves were so wet and slippery that I refused to take a step further and was left behind by the adults to wander, alone and lost, through alleys that were like tunnels to a child. The dread of those moments stayed inside me, coming back to me in any graveyard I visited after that. The one next to our house was my father's. Just as my mother belonged in the kitchen, my father belonged in the graveyard.

Yuko Tsushima

At some time or another, I had come by the knowledge that my father died in water, not on land. I guess I picked that up the way children do. When I was about ten, I also learned the difficult word *jusui* ('entering water'), an indirect term for suicide by drowning. It was a weight off my mind to think that my father hadn't died on land. To me, a death on land and a death in water were not the same thing. Dying underwater didn't count.

My mother has left her umbrella behind again. She is in her seventies, it's true, but she gives the impression she'll be going strong for another thirty years, if not forty. Why is it always her umbrella she forgets? It drives me nuts. I keep seeing it out of the corner of my eye, every day, in the stand just inside the front door, yet I haven't even let her know I have it, and it certainly never occurs to me to take it to her. I just leave it sitting there.

The long black plastic handle of that one umbrella juts out of the stand it shares with mine and my child's, leaning at an angle, cluttering up the narrow hallway. Preferring to have as little as possible to do with my mother's umbrella, I leave it there – and this makes me all the more aware of being stuck with it.

There was another umbrella of hers I ended up keeping like that. Seeing as how she has no way of getting them back unless she happens to notice them herself when she comes over, they're obviously going to remain on my hands; but, unable to bring it up, I've carted that first umbrella along each

10

time I've moved, and eventually, in exasperation, I've hidden it someplace out of my sight.

I expect she has missed the latest one, but it apparently never dawns on her that she left it in her daughter's apartment. Or is she so sure she couldn't have that she won't even ask?

It is, admittedly, a silly thing to care about. Which is why it irks me.

Perhaps, in a generous gesture, she wants me to have the umbrella she knows she left at my place. One can never have too many umbrellas, yet they're actually quite expensive to buy, thus it will be a great help to her daughter, who, let's face it, is still leading the kind of life where an umbrella, once broken, never gets repaired.

If that is how she sees it, then I don't want her to think I'm being stubborn over some old umbrella out of pride, and I'm equally afraid of letting myself in for an earful of personal comments of this kind by returning it to her. I can see myself blowing my top, and that's what I'm afraid of.

Or maybe, in her old age, she is protecting herself by ruling out the very idea of such a lapse. It's true she's never been forgetful; even now, she never leaves anything else behind. It's only umbrellas so far. Hence, perhaps, her reluctance to think she could have been absentminded. Especially not at that scatterbrain of a daughter's, the one she always used to scold for forgetting things; perhaps, in her view, the umbrella has therefore simply evaporated.

I can't tell what she is really thinking. Maybe, like me, she is bothered by it but can't say anything, for fear of a daughter who is liable to blow her top over an umbrella. I have never once understood my mother's feelings. At all. And so I can't return a lousy umbrella.

On rainy Sundays, my mother remembers her daughter, who left her dreams in the care of some man who already had a wife and family and is now bringing up the child of that involvement on her own, and she sets out from the house where she, too, lives alone. If it's still raining when she starts for home again, she will take her umbrella. Sometimes it will have stopped and she'll leave the umbrella with her daughter. That umbrella disturbs and frightens her daughter, while she herself is disturbed and frightened at having forgotten it. When it's nothing, really. When it really doesn't mean a thing.

. . . Water. I was forever wishing that human beings could live without it. Just once, I would have liked to tell that so-and-so water who was mistress in my house. I hated the trudge to the local well and back. With a small child and a baby in the house, I had to fetch water many times a day, no matter how sparingly I used it. If everybody had been in the same situation, I could have resigned myself to it, but ours was among the few houses in those days still relying on a well; and, as if to rub in the drudgery, it was a communal well at that. If only we'd had a yard with a private well, then as long as it didn't rain I could have done the laundry there in peace and quiet, and we could have washed our hands and feet at the well side. I expect I wouldn't have minded that, as I was accustomed to it in my childhood. It wasn't so much the cramped conditions that I resented, though. Those I was prepared for. This was Tokyo, after all; I was no longer in the provinces. But I was at least counting on running water to make up for it. It never occurred to me that we mightn't have running water. However, the house that my husband blithely decided to rent shared a well: one well among ten houses in two facing rows, and, to crown it all, ours was the furthest away. Even in provincial towns like the one I came from, piped water was no longer a rarity by then. So in that new suburban tract on the outskirts of Tokyo, you had the worst inconveniences of the country combined with the disadvantages of the city. If we'd lived in the mountains, say, we could have gone for days without seeing anyone, and a river or tarn would have done me for water. Living right in the heart of Tokyo itself is quite like living in the mountains – in the midst of so many people, one hardly sees anyone, and the tap water, the fountains and the ponds, they're all mine. But in that house there was no water I could call my own.

I learned for the first time how much water weighs. As I fetched it from the well, it was so heavy something seemed to be wrong. Why did it weigh such a ton? Because you weren't supposed to carry water like that; it was supposed to flow on its own. From beneath the ground, Suijin, the Water Deity, was trying to seize it back, demanding to know what I meant to do with it, and it was her pulling on it that was weighing it down. She'd have me sinking into the ground with it if I didn't watch out. Afraid of the weight, are you? Then drop it! she snapped, as I panted and reeled under those loads, day in and day out, through heat and snow, rain and wind. But I kept on, never so much as pausing between the well and the house. If I put the water down, I muttered to myself, I'd never get it back. I couldn't obey Suijin. We needed that water. Our lives depended on it.

With the water I fetched day after day, I rinsed the rice, made miso soup, did the laundry, sponged myself. And gradually my belly filled out and a baby was born. She was our third. She was the only one of the three who was born in that house. I'd gone to my parents' to have the others, and their house had proper running water, even though it was in the provinces. It had a bath, I'll have you know.

Another baby meant more water. I continued to haul it from the well. The baby did just fine, even if that was the only water she knew. Before long, she was crawling around the little house; she learned to sit up and to stand. Our oldest started school. The middle one, though his birthplace hadn't lacked for water, was a strange child for some reason, still crawling at the age of four. It was like having two babies. Two babies' worth of dribbling. Two babies' worth of nappies. Of heat rash in the summers, and illnesses. The quantities of water I carried horrified me. It was never enough, and I was at a loss to understand why. Sometimes I thought what fools we humans are – it's living on land that causes all these woes; if we need water so badly we should just return to it, then we'd be set, wouldn't we? As I drew water at the well, I'd be thinking that if the pump were removed there'd be a hole through which we could return.

Then, one day, my husband did return to the water. I had always kept an eye on him – he couldn't do anything right by himself – and when I let Suijin distract me, it was him, not me, whom the water swallowed. I'll admit that, at the time, the Water Deity was taking up more of my attention than my husband; but still, where in heaven's name did she get an idea like that? It's true he'd gone off with another woman, it's true he'd fathered a child with her, it's true he couldn't look me in the face, and I admit that each time he strayed, I choked with rage and complained what a dreadful man and disastrous husband he was till my head was ready to split, but that doesn't mean I hated him. He was the man I loved.

The water was a rain-swollen stream near our house. After several days, the drowned bodies of my husband and a certain woman surfaced together. But what did I care about those things? That ugly corpse was not my husband. Suijin had merely delivered up the cast-off shell to the land.

I glowered at her and demanded: What did you whisper to my husband? What did you show him under the water?

Oh, she was in fine fettle, sending downpours, drawing the stream's muddy torrent up into a waterspout, soaking me to the skin. Grieve all you like, she taunted. Cry your eyes out. Wail till your throat's on fire. You can't escape water – look, you're drenched in it. You can have your fill. There's nothing else here. The place is awash. Your husband is water now. You are married to water. You will be deafened by its voice, shattered by its weight.

I glared steadily at Suijin, with none of the grief and fear

15

she expected. What she didn't know was that, when you hand them something they don't want to accept, human beings turn into hollow, transparent, oblivious creatures. That glare gave me the space to keep breathing. I heard the water's roar but I wasn't deafened. I went on carrying the well water, soaked and stranded as I was. I saw the women who used the same well, huddles of them, but I saw them through water. The road and the other houses were on the far side, too. My worried brother, who showed up almost daily, and even my children were cut off by it. It was clouded and frothing, and it made it hard to see what lay beyond.

But I could still breathe. It came to me suddenly: I wasn't underwater. There were some things Suijin didn't have it in her power to do. I groped in the water before my eyes and dragged the children's bodies to my breast. They were warm, they smelled of sunshine. Hugging them to me, for the first time I lay down and closed my eyes.

Soon, instead of facing down the Water Deity, I found myself having to return the stares of other people. All their sympathy, all their kind offers amounted to nothing more than ghoulish curiosity. Not to mention condescension. I didn't have it in me to humour them politely. They'd probably been watching our house already – sensing something brewing – while my husband was alive, but there would be no holding back now that he was gone: 'My dear, what you need is a good old heart-to-heart, woman to woman, just say the word if there's anything we can do, that's what neighbours are for, don't go brooding all alone.' Given the chance, they'd have barged in and made even my children dance to their tune. I glared at the women from the alley when I went to the well, and if one of them dared speak to me, I gritted my teeth and looked away with a shudder. I took to locking my door. And all at once, I was the villain. I don't know what the women in those cheek-by-jowl houses whispered among themselves. The very thought of it made me feel dirty.

There was no point in staying. It galled me to let people think I had run away, but protecting myself from those idle women was a chore I could do without. I went to my brother's at first; he was living in Tokyo, having sold the house he'd inherited in our hometown. We'd been close since we were children, I could feel at ease with him. And the house where he lived on his own had indoor running water – all you could want, chlorinated and clean, at the turn of a tap. I burst into tears at the sight of the gushing spout. I bawled out loud.

My brother seemed indignant. 'All this time, in that house, you've had to cry quietly, haven't you?'

I laughed through my sobs, 'No, it's the water. Appearing just like that – it startled me.'

Life at my brother's was free from care. And Suijin never appeared out of the tap. I only wished we could stay there for good. Now that my husband had gone to the Water Deity, my brother was the only close male relative my children had. And they were so very young. With him at my side, I could have been my old self again, the brave big sister who took her timid little brother firmly in hand when we were children. He was six years my junior, a darling boy

with big eyes in a pale face; for a long time he had been my
pet and my pride. I bossed him about – some might say
'bullied'. I gave him motherly hugs when the tears rolled
down his cheeks, and he was just so adorable I had to pull
his hair and tug his earlobes. But he was fond of me. Even
after he'd grown up and gone away, he still regarded me
with those same eyes whenever we met.

However, I couldn't take up residence at my brother's with
the children. What people made of a sister in her thirties and
a brother in his twenties under the same roof I don't know,
but it would have been a shame to let the nasty rumours
surrounding me, and maybe new ones, shadow the life of
my brother, who was single and a very intelligent young man
pursuing postgraduate studies. As the son who had inherited
our late parents' property, which was the way in those days,
he was a young man with a positively radiant outlook.

In the end, I took the children and moved on after barely
a month. My brother had arranged for me to receive a share
of the estate, persuading the family that these were special
circumstances; even so, he continued to worry about how I
would get by. He had also arranged to have my middle child
examined at a university hospital. Ashamed to depend on
him at every turn, I couldn't help sounding grudgingly impa-
tient to be going. He was very much against my moving out
and wound up protesting tearfully: 'Why such stubborn
pride? What does it matter that I'm younger than you? You'll
always be my big sister. But these days your little brother is
a man with pretty good prospects, so let me take care of you.'

The more he talked like this, the more it stung to have to turn to him. Yet, in actual fact, there was nothing else I could do.

In time, my middle child – who had been diagnosed as incurably intellectually handicapped – did start to walk, and the baby was growing up, turning three, then four. Before I knew it, each day with the children had become a deep joy.

The old house I had decided to make our home was at the end of a lane, next to a graveyard. It was ideal for keeping to ourselves and not being bothered. It had running water, naturally, and indeed a bath, which not even my brother's house had. I put in flower beds. The flowers were such a treat, each an eyeful of colour. I marvelled at how green stems and earth-covered roots could produce such pretty hues. In the summer, I let my two youngest bathe in a wooden tub in the garden. They were as excited as could be, splashing in those few inches of sun-warmed water. Around them, the dahlias and sunflowers and zinnias were blooming. In the autumn, it was the asters, and in winter, as I sat in the enclosed veranda darning or knitting sweaters for the children, the sasanqua camellia was in bloom, and the adonises. In the balmy light, I was content.

Around that time, my husband's relations in his distant hometown began to send modest sums of money for the children. I myself gradually began to take in work that I could do at home. My brother was due to get married. I wanted to do whatever I could for him, though in the end there wasn't much I could do, lest my efforts undermine his young wife's confidence. After his marriage, our visits to each other's homes grew infrequent, but that was nothing to fret about, either.

It was quiet there, at the end of the alley, where no one bothered us. I felt no need of any company but the children's. And by my side was where they liked to be. They didn't go far to play, and they didn't ask to bring friends home. We had one another, the three children and me. Just the four of us.

They were all obedient children, good to their mother. Not once did I find them too much of a handful. My middle child began to be cared for during the day at an institution. He was such an innocent boy, a boy like spring sunshine; he would bring a smile to anyone's lips. The eldest blossomed – and she had brains, as well as beauty. She was a quiet, reasonable girl. The youngest, too, was an amiable child, who never made a fuss. They all loved their mother dearly and did their best to shield me from the prying and gossiping outside world.

We could look up at the moon through the bathroom window. What bliss it was to gaze at the moon while soaking in the tub with the younger two. I needed nothing more. I used to ask myself if there'd ever been such happiness.

My children. How fast they grew. Getting too big for tricycles, learning to ride bikes. The roof of that old house leaked badly when it rained. We positioned basins, pans, rice pots, and bowls on the tatami, till it took some ingenuity to lay out the futons when we wanted to go to bed. The children were delighted, of course. Different plinks echoed through the room, some low-pitched, some high. The biggest drips spattered water around the containers, while others slowly formed droplets that fell at steady intervals.

The children turn everything into a game. They'll switch receptacles and listen to the different sounds, or take a basin away then whisk it back at the last moment. Just when I think I'll never get them settled, there'll be a hush and I'll find them fast asleep, looking cosier there among the drips than on a rainless night.

Much later, after attending to a number of tasks, I get into bed myself. I turn off the light and the house is dark. The drips reverberate as if to beat against me. The children's breathing is faintly audible. The drips constantly seem about to tail away, yet they never let up. I close my eyes. The dripping rain pelts down in drops of every size. I make myself small. It streams down on me. I try to calm my pounding heart: Go to sleep now, you must sleep. The water becomes a muddy torrent. The torrent embraces me. I twist and let out a moan. The water is heavy. Oh, not again. My body will shatter. It's the Water Deity up to her old tricks. What about the children? she murmurs. They haven't noticed this water yet, have they?

The children are asleep beyond the water, which is always flowing quietly beside them.

. . . My intellectually handicapped brother died, and many years later I became a mother myself. I have one child, a boy. An ordinary boy, not like my brother. I didn't visit the grave that holds my father's and my brother's ashes, either before or after my son was born. I don't know whether my mother does.

She sometimes comes to see me. The sight of her face puts me on my guard, a habit I've had since childhood. She sighs at this: just because her daughter has foolishly ended up with a child she insists on bringing up alone, does she really have to spring to his defence with that wild look? Better be careful not to rile her, though, because she's a wounded bear with a cub. My mother's expression says all this when she comes to visit. She looks around to see how she can please me. She wants to do something – anything – for her daughter: to put the girl at ease, because she's obviously struggling, and her child's situation is a worry, and surely the natural thing would be for her to come back to the family that awaits with open arms. My mother continues to live alone (despite my married sister being nearby) and to wait for the day I come back.

Just yesterday, she brought over several dishes she'd cooked for dinner. The trip takes her thirty minutes by bus but I can't tell her not to come, if that's what she wants to do. In her old age, she wants to be a mother who puts her daughter's welfare before her own.

Around the meal table, the three of us are limited to the most humdrum topics. And even then I watch my tongue, because a single misstep would encourage her belief that I'm floundering. The child is the only one who chats away, saying the first thing that pops into his head.

'Granny,' he began last night as another thought occurred to him, 'you're actually scary, aren't you?'

My mother answered with a broad smile, 'Not a bit. I'm your kind old granny, you know that.'

'Eat up and don't chatter.' I spoke sharply, on tenterhooks. I had a feeling I knew what was coming.

'What makes you think I'm scary?' asked my old mother, perturbed.

''Cos Mum says you hit her. You hit her with a stick, right?' He spoke unconcernedly, looking amused. I glared at him in utter dismay.

Dumbfounded for a moment, my mother then let slip a wry smile. 'What nonsense . . .'

'But Mum said!' the child insisted with increasing glee as he took in the effect his words had had on the adults. Unable by now to hold up my head, I fixed my eyes on my lap.

My old mother replied casually, however, with another wry smile, 'Of course it isn't true. Do you really think your granny is capable of doing such a thing?'

After considering a little, the child said brightly, 'Then it's a lie. So that's it.'

'Yes, it's a silly story.'

'Mum told a li-ie,' he jeered at me. 'Why did you tell a lie?'

My mother tried to close the subject, her tone conveying that she was too shocked to talk about it. 'Goodness knows . . . Now, eat your veggies.'

Let it go, I told myself, as she was attempting to do. She

didn't want an ancient embarrassment raked up in front of the child. But I couldn't stay silent.

'I wouldn't lie about something like that.' Taken aback by the emotion in my voice, the child looked back and forth at his grandmother and me. I went on shakily, 'It's true.'

My old mother gave a sad sigh. 'Is that right . . . Leave it, will you?'

We fell silent. It was all I could do to stop myself seizing her by the lapels, shouting and doing who knows what else, so I kept out of her way in case meeting her eyes set me off. Instead I tackled a load of clean laundry, folding it slowly and inefficiently in a corner until she went home. She did the clearing up, then quietly let herself out without a word to me or the child, who was watching television.

This left me wondering confusedly whether she truly didn't remember. If so, how hurt she must have been. I could see the figure she must have presented, walking the dark streets alone in a daze, her age very evident. She would be spending sleepless nights again, moaning in sorrow and pain. And I, in turn, was stunned at this mother of mine.

I had indeed told the child. It was in answer to his saying that I was scary but Granny was kind.

'That's because your own child matters so much. No one who's bringing up a child can be all smiley all the time. Granny was a really scary mum. If I didn't do what I was told, I got hit. Sometimes with a stick. But of course she's kind to her grandchild. I can be soft on a child, too, if he's not mine to bring up.'

I had thought at the time that those memories must be uncomfortable for my mother now that she'd set her heart on being a kind granny, but the possibility that she'd clean forgotten had never crossed my mind. It was inconceivable to me. *That* mother was the only one I had. This old woman who cooed to my child and looked out for me was not my mother.

My mother constantly lost control of herself and struck me. But not my older siblings: perhaps I was a child she could vent her feelings on. She needed an outlet. Someplace to let herself go.

With my sister, who remembered her father, she was never sure what to do. My intellectually handicapped brother she practically idolized. And me? I was a child who didn't know her father, a child who was all hers. A child on her own side, born not long before the one he'd fathered somewhere else. An average child, healthy, heedless, engrossed in play. Whatever the reason, I must have been her only safety valve. If a slap for dawdling set my nose bleeding, I'd receive another because she didn't like the nosebleed. Once I hid all her rulers (or so I thought), hoping to stop her at least using them on me; for this I was again hit with a ruler, on the shoulders and the rear. I scrambled to escape these hidings, as any child would, because they hurt. But I didn't think about why I'd been hit, and so I kept on doing the things that made her mad. All I ever learned was to fear her.

Though afraid, I was a child who instantly forgot what I was told. I couldn't be trusted with errands, I'd leave my satchel at school, I was in no hurry to do my homework, of course, and I'd forget the time when playing at a friend's place. My mother had ample opportunity to get angry.

She provided herself with bamboo canes the right size for my growing body. I fled her more than ever, learning to disguise awkward facts with lies. I was once clouted in front of a friend, who had come to ask me around to her place, for saying I wanted to go. Oh, so my home wasn't good enough for me? Had I no shame? she demanded. Where was my pride?

Shameless: she always called me that. I never understood why, and I had no answer. But I no longer cried or said I was sorry, and a child who wouldn't apologize irritated her all the more. I may not have known what she meant, but a mother's words leave their mark. Wondering if I was shameless, I spent my free time at my school friends' homes – anywhere but my own.

The punishments didn't let up even when I reached middle school; in fact, as my brother died not long after that, they became more intense. She stopped raising her hand to me only after I pushed her to the floor, unable to endure it any longer. From then on, she tended to stay in her room and say nothing. And I grew distant from her; I was beyond caring about winning over this stern mother of mine. But my fear was ingrained. All these years later, I remain wary, still afraid of her.

Yet, hard as I find it to believe, she has apparently forgotten what she was once like. Perhaps I should forget, too, and feel easier around my elderly mother – or so I tell myself, but a visceral reaction can't be changed at will. That mother was mine. A mother who hated and feared the outside world as she held her children tight, and who faced that world with disdain, adamant that no one was going to look down on her: that's who raised me. I grew up tutored in what happened if you trusted outsiders, taught that solitude was the only weapon of defence. Though I have to say, I was a child who never made any effort to understand how my mother felt.

I slept badly myself that night. The thought of her lying awake – thinking sadly and bitterly how I must hate her to tell such a dreadful lie, yet reminding herself that I was her daughter, whom she loved – was never far from my mind.

And I dreamed that I returned her umbrella. Neither she nor it appeared in the dream, but that was evidently what I had gone to do. I did all the talking.

. . . I don't want to see your blasted umbrella. You think I'm that easy to scare? I know your methods. What I can't bear is that you've mixed up my troubles and yours and you won't admit it. No, it's no use going 'What nonsense' and looking sad. Just think about it: why do you trouble yourself so much over me? Why do you brood over me and fear me, yet turn to me? And why always when it rains? You hear the rain and you picture me all alone, afraid of the rising waters, my child in my arms. Trapped, unable even to weep. But that's yourself you're seeing, not me. You feel moved to tears and you think they're for my sake, so you come to check up on me – not on my sister, who has a proper husband and was never entirely yours anyway. But then all you get from me are dirty looks. No clinging and no reassurances. So you're bewildered and afraid of me. And I'm afraid of you. So afraid, I don't know what to do.

You've always viewed me through your own troubles. Can you deny it? People depend on their misfortunes. We curse them, but actually we're wedded to them, proud of them even. And you're no exception. You're afraid of the water that stole your husband, but all you can do is consort with it. It's always around you. As far as you're concerned, he didn't die, he turned to water. What happens on land vanishes in water, and the reverse is true, too. Water is your greatest fear, but the world of water is also where your deepest prayers find a hearing. Away from that realm and its deity, you lose sight of the feelings you still have for your husband; they become lost in your feelings as a mother. And you think I'm like you. You believe that as we're both in Suijin's power, it's only natural to listen together to her voice, feel her weight together. And so you leave your umbrella at my place. I know that seems far-fetched, but it's you who puts the idea in my head, dragging that water everywhere you go. It scares me. I'm afraid I'll go under.

And you're afraid of me, too. Because I came bumbling along right when the Water Deity was calling your husband, and I sounded a lot like her when I wailed. And then there was his other child, so the wailing nearly deafened you. When you lashed out with a stick, it wasn't at me. You were fighting your pain in the shape of Suijin. You weren't seeing me, so you don't think you ever laid a finger on me. Is that it?

I'm past hating you for it now. That was the only mother I knew growing up, so I couldn't love any other kind. There you were, your eyes on the realm of water, never a glance to spare for anyone on land, shielding yourself with disdain.

But now that you're getting on in years, although you're still afraid of me, you'd like to forget the reason why. You fancy yourself as a cooing, gooey, vanilla grandmother. Don't be ridiculous. I'd like to slap your cheeks till I get through to you. Listen, you were never an indulgent mother and you never looked out for me. I won't have you feeling sorry for me or your grandson. You don't get to think, If only my poor daughter would let me help her out.

You're convinced everything would be fine if we lived together. If only we could. But you live in a world I don't recognize. What a halcyon glow our childhood must have for you. Your eldest so capable, the little ones like a couple of playful, tumbling puppies. We came at your call and clung passionately to you. Your flower beds bloomed, and we loved to wear the sweaters you knitted us. We adored your snacks, we slept on your hand-sewn futons. Your children. You were surrounded by their bubbly laughter, their round cheeks shining with health. You were their queen. Their sweet fragrance enveloped you. Everything in sight glittered a dazzling gold. When spring breezes blew, the light streamed through the air. It was a place of such beauty. Such happiness.

You're intoxicated with that beauty, and you believe you can regain it. But why would that idyll materialize now, when it never existed in the first place? You couldn't even set the stage after all this time. My brother has died, my sister and I ceased to be children over twenty years ago, and even the old house has gone.

Your dream is bound to end as a dream.

That's the way it is, sad and unfair as it may seem. So you're better off with the dream. I can't live with you, because the dream is all you have. You live in a fantasy. I don't want to go bursting that bubble now.

A Dragon Palace. You're enchanted by a Dragon Palace of your very own. That beautiful realm where a hundred days are a hundred years. A tranquil haven in the deep, suffused with a light unimaginable on land. In the years to come, that light will steadily grow clearer and stronger, the watery realm will grow more beautiful in your eyes, and you will enter that realm.

That's how I hope it will be. Because I love you. And I don't want to think that one day you will die.

Ah, that reminds me. I have to tell my five-year-old about the Dragon Palace – to tell him that, somewhere in the deep, the original of that underwater castle he's so proud of surely exists. There, as colourful fish tickle the tips of their noses, the folk we long to see again sleep the sleep in which a hundred days are a hundred years.

Of Dogs and Walls

In a town whose name escapes me, I came across a small park with a freestanding wall in one corner. Brick, I seem to remember, or maybe concrete. I paused before it, expecting some sort of inscription, and saw instead an oddly shaped hole in the middle. It wasn't immediately obvious what the shape was, but then it came to me: it was a human form. A figure in mid-stride, one arm swung forward, the other back. There was something tongue-in-cheek about it that set one giggling while puzzling over what it was doing there.

I later remarked on the curious sight to a friend and asked, 'What do you suppose it was?'

'From what I've heard,' she said at once, 'it's an artist's rendering of this fictional character, the Walker-through-Walls. Why did he walk through walls? Can't help you there, I'm afraid. You'll have to read the story. "Le passe-muraille", I believe it's called.'

This made me think instantly of Perry, who belonged to my mother years ago. If you ask me, he slipped through a wall, too, when he entered my mother's life. I wouldn't put it past him.

Without mentioning it, her mother – on her own now that she herself had left home – had acquired a dog. This was Perry. She claimed he had just turned up in the yard, clearly a stray, and so she'd decided to keep him. But there was no hole in the wall. Unlike those old wooden fences that had gaps everywhere, the wall of precast concrete around the house was utterly impervious. Her mother wasn't in the habit of leaving the gate open, either; that would be unsafe. And there was no way the dog could have slipped under a gate set so close to the ground. All of which meant that it was nigh on impossible for a stray simply to have turned up on the property. Ownerless dogs roaming the neighbourhood were a thing of the past, anyway. Could her mother have brought him back from somewhere? Still, how could she have come by a fully grown animal like that, and where?

By the time the daughter noticed, the dog named Perry was making himself at home, cool as you please, in the old kennel that had housed the dogs before him. The tin bowls he ate and drank from, and even his collar and chain, had been theirs.

'Perry – as in Commodore Perry, of the Black Ships?'

Her mother nodded without enthusiasm. 'What of it?' said her look. She wasn't one to bother much over naming a pet, though she did seem to be convinced for some reason that dogs should have Western names: the last one had been Louis, the one before that Jack, and before him there was Mickey. So 'Perry' was an equally casual choice. But this carelessly named Perry had become part of her day-to-day life there on her own. And he remained her companion, living to quite an age.

Her mother didn't dote on Perry noticeably and never brought him up in conversation. Yet you could say she cared for him, the daughter supposed, since she fed him regularly and let him off the chain at night, giving him the run of the yard for his own exercise and her security, and Perry for his part could be said to trust her as dogs do. The daughter perhaps resented Perry's bond with her mother, unreasonably enough, considering she had moved out. When she visited, she never attempted to pat the dog chained beside his kennel, and he ignored her in return. He was black, a mixed breed, medium size, with no other distinguishing characteristics. He was probably a quiet dog by nature, as he never bothered her with his barking.

It was the fact that her mother had taken on a dog without her knowing that rankled. She liked to think that sooner or later he would wander off the way he had come, but Perry would not oblige. Although they couldn't say exactly how old he was, since no one knew when he had been born, over the years he grew to be quite old by any measure. When he went, it wouldn't be before his time.

On one of her visits to her mother, there was no sign of him in the kennel.

The daughter, by now in her forties, asked, 'Where's Perry?' She knew the answer.

'He died the other day,' her mother replied simply and without obvious sadness, and the daughter, too, left it at that. She didn't ask what her mother had done with Perry's body. Maybe she'd contacted the sanitation department. That was probably it, because at her age – she had not worked for many years – she surely wasn't strong enough to dig a hole in the garden and bury him herself.

After Perry died, the daughter was, if anything, more aware of him than before whenever she saw the bags of dog food, collar and chain on a dusty shelf by the side door, and the kennel in the corner of the garden, yet the sight also irked her: why didn't her mother get rid of that stuff? Still, she could hardly go ahead and do it herself. Her mother might be keeping the collar and the kennel because she was grieving deeply, or she might have merely forgotten; both seemed equally possible, and the daughter couldn't tell.

She had been only ten when the family moved to the house her mother would later share with Perry.

One morning a day or two before the move, when the old house that was their previous home must have been in chaos with the packing, she'd looked out from its veranda into what should have been the yard and boggled at the unaccustomed vista that met her eyes. On a closer view, the one change turned out to be that the wooden fence had been pushed over from the outside, exposing the alley. The fence had been remarkably flimsy, half rotted away already by the looks of it. The ten-year-old had been shocked and let down to find they'd been ensconced inside such a paper-thin fence. The old house was destined to be demolished once they'd moved, and after her mother had pointed out which trees she wanted taken to the new place, the gardener apparently had arrived first thing and, in his zeal, knocked down the fence to allow direct access between the alley and the garden.

The old house was old indeed: built by her grandparents

before the war, it had survived the air raids that devastated much of Tokyo. Feeling sentimental on hearing that it was due to come down, the daughter had got out her camera, a hand-me-down from a cousin, and taken a number of photos. It was only when she saw them developed after the move that she noticed the whole house was listing. It had such a lean it looked ready to give way at the slightest push; she wondered how she'd been unaware of it till now. There really was nothing for it but to knock the old place down, she conceded, which seemed to put her regrets to rest. For a long time, though, she constantly returned to the old house in her dreams.

The daughter would later have no memory of the packing and carrying, which must mean she'd done precious little to help. At the end, the family headed for the new house in a taxi. She held the black cat they called Kuro, while Jack the dog was held by her brother, Toru-chan. Although he was older and the diminutive was out of place, she was allowed to call him 'chan' because he had a developmental disability. She didn't address him as *oniisan* ('older brother') in the usual way. Not that she ever babied him by dropping the 'chan' or shortening his name; she saw herself as showing the proper respect by always calling him 'Toru-chan' in full. He called her by her name only, as a big brother was entitled to do.

What fun it was to be crammed together in the taxi, tightly restraining Kuro and Jack who, terrified by their first ride in a car, were struggling to escape if given half a chance. Toru-chan and his little sister would look at each other and laugh, bump shoulders and laugh. It was midsummer, and since taxis in those days had no air-conditioning they had to keep the windows wound down. She seemed to remember it was when they braked for a red light that Kuro bolted out of her arms.

'Oops, Kuro got away, can I go after him?' she appealed to her mother in the front seat.

Her mother peered out of her window. 'Leave it for now, we'll find him later. Don't worry, he's sure to go back and hang around the old house.'

That seemed fair enough, but for the rest of the ride the sister still felt miserably at fault, fretting that Kuro might stay lost. He never did turn up, in fact, and was presumed to have found a new home somewhere in their old neighbourhood. Though she wasn't sure just how hard the grownups had actually looked, she didn't make the trip and search herself, and from then on would guiltily avoid the subject of the missing Kuro. Besides, she'd had good reason to let the situation with Kuro slide, considering what happened that night, or perhaps it was the next. They were all busy unpacking and tidying away when Jack, excited by the unfamiliar surroundings, slipped his collar, ran out into the street through the gateway – which had not yet been fitted with a gate – and was hit head-on by a large truck.

The sister, in pursuit, was just in time to witness the collision. Startled by the looming truck, Jack dropped to his haunches and raised his face. The bumper clipped him on the forehead, the truck sped off, and he lay in the road unmarked, killed instantly, his skull fractured. The sister fetched her mother and her cousin, a student who had come to lend a hand and was staying the night. He carried Jack's body in from the road and buried it in a hole he dug in the garden. In the midsummer heat it would have quickly started to decompose. Toru-chan and his sister watched him work from a little distance. She was crying, Toru-chan was not.

A month or so later, Toru-chan took a spade and set to work digging up the place where Jack was buried. His sister spotted him, yelled, 'No! Stop that!' and snatched the spade away. Most likely Toru-chan was simply vexed that Jack was hidden in the ground. Puzzled at what Jack was doing confined in there, Toru-chan wanted to have a look, while to the sister, who could guess that the corpse would be putrefying in the earth by now, to see Jack in such a dreadful state was unthinkable. Toru-chan couldn't understand why she was thwarting his efforts to let Jack out. But if his beloved sister didn't like him doing something, he thought he'd better stop.

With Kuro lost and Jack gone, they were left with the kennel that the carpenter who built the new house had made them as an extra from scraps of timber. It was exceptionally solid, being a house builder's handiwork, and massive – they couldn't move it by themselves from where he'd placed it. Jack had been another mongrel, middle-sized, with a brown coat. As they had kept him collarless in a chicken-wire run at the old house, a kennel was a novelty for the family and might well have been fairly disconcerting to Jack, had he lived in it.

Whether loth to let such a fine kennel go to waste or feeling in need of a guard dog, their mother then brought home a white pointer with black spots that she'd bought at a pet shop.

She explained to Toru-chan and his sister that he came from a breed of intelligent hunting dogs, and she named him Louis, pronounced 'Louie'. Delighted with the lively new puppy, the children let him into their beds, much to their mother's displeasure, and set about quasi-training him, teaching him to sit, shake hands and fetch sticks and balls, but when Toru-chan suddenly passed away, neither his little sister nor their mother could spare much thought for Louis, who developed heartworm some time later and, his coughing and wheezing scarcely heeded by the family, at length curled up and died. Even so, he had been alive during her secondary-school years. She gave him a burial near Jack.

What caught the ten-year-old sister's eye in the neighbourhood they'd moved into were the walled enclosures wherever she looked. The taxi ride from the old house had taken about twenty minutes, and she and Toru-chan would be commuting by tram to their schools, now that the distance was too far to walk. The children weren't told how their mother had located the new property. But she must have been delighted to say goodbye to the slug-infested kitchen, with its cave crickets and its mice scrabbling in the ceiling, and to the cold dark privy, at long last. She had managed to build up the business she'd taken over, with a brother's help, after her husband's early death; and now that even her son with the intellectual disability was a twelve-year-old middle-school pupil – albeit in a special class – they could probably get along without the part-time housekeeper she'd had to hire. It must have seemed to her, with apologies to her late husband, as if they'd come out the other side of the crisis that had started when she found herself alone with the children.

The first wall that awaited at their destination was a gloomy brick affair nearly ten feet tall.

'There's a prison!' the sister said.

Her mother said reprovingly, 'That's no prison. There's a garden inside that wall.'

The sister nodded, unconvinced; a ten-foot-high brick wall surrounding a garden made no real sense to her. She eventually learned that the garden had belonged to a feudal lord's Edo residence when their mother took them there, maybe six months or a year later. But as they were making their way towards the exit on that occasion, the sister heard two or three boys chorus 'There's no cure for a foo-ool' from behind a clump of azaleas, and a chill went through her. That was half the proverb; they were leaving out the part 'till he dies'. It must have been classmates of hers who knew of Toru-chan's existence. Her mother and Toru-chan ambled on along the gravel path, seemingly unhearing. Just like that, the sister was put off the garden for good, and she never overcame her aversion to the brick wall, either.

Almost every house in that part of town was surrounded by a wall. These were mostly of precast concrete, plain grey in colour, but some were capped with tiers of old-fashioned tiles, still others were whitewashed and topped with Western-style blue roofs, and a few were even jaggedly burglar-proofed with embedded glass and coils of barbed wire. In their former

39

neighbourhood, many houses had not been fenced, much less walled, and such fences as there were had been old wooden ones like their own.

After moving in, Toru-chan and his little sister roamed the nearby streets with keen interest. Every street-front wall had a gate, but there were side entrances to be found, too – usually a small wooden door which, on being pushed, would often prove to be unlocked. Letting herself into other people's gardens and trespassing for no reason was not something the ten-year-old sister would ever have got up to on her own, but it was possible with Toru-chan in tow. For even when they were caught, if the angry homeowner noticed his appearance they would be forgiven. 'Oh, I see, it's no good telling him,' the stranger would say, and perhaps even add a kind word: 'It must be hard on you having to mind this one.' The little sister, for better or worse, could make that sort of calculation. But sheer curiosity impelled Toru-chan's actions: if there was a wall, he wanted to see what was beyond it. To Toru-chan – and of course to his little sister at his side – this was the best fun there was.

One door opened on to row upon row of many-hued roses, all in bloom. She recalled the rose garden extending out of sight in every direction, but it couldn't have; it had probably just seemed so vast to a child's eyes. Behind another door, they set a yard full of chickens squawking. The owner came running at the rooster's raucous cock-a-doodle-doo. There were still people who kept chickens in the middle of Tokyo in those days. Once they almost walked slap into a man washing a blue car. A broken swing stirred in the wind in one garden; another had a bed of white pebbles with standing stone lanterns, just like a temple.

The existence of a boy next door began to register on the little sister after she turned eleven. Some remark of her mother's about the neighbours' circumstances brought him to her attention. But where could her mother have heard about them? Not directly, surely, as there were no signs of a growing friendship with the lady of the house. Next door's father had also died young, which had forced them to sell half of their sizable plot; the widowed wife and her only son now lived at the back, on the remainder of the land, behind the new occupants. The young master was her own age. The glimpses she caught from time to time over the wall showed him to be pale and thin, his features not especially chiselled or handsome. Maybe it was her imagination, but he seemed very shy and highly strung.

Set into the concrete wall between their two houses there was a little wicket door, so low that an adult would have had to duck to pass through. It appeared to have gone unopened for many years, indeed to be nailed shut from the other side, and was patchy with rust and dark mouldering stains along the bottom of the wood. A leafy fatsia shrub had been planted in front of it, which accounted for her not having noticed it before. The weeds were thick back there, too. Though their house was new, the wall had been there a long time.

She asked her mother why there was a door in the wall.

'It seems it was put there as an emergency escape route in

the old days. You know, in case of fire,' came the answer. 'But times have changed and it'd just be awkward, and unsafe, if it was always flying open. So it's a "forbidden door".'

The forbidden door and the young master became a source of fascination for the sister. These feelings would have meant nothing to Toru-chan. Knowing this, she didn't inform him of the low door that led to the neighbours' place. If she had, he would immediately have tried to jemmy it open. She wanted to protect her fascination, or her dream, from Toru-chan. It was hers alone, and it was embarrassing; she didn't want her mother to find out, either. Sometimes she parted the leaves and gave the door a gingerly push or tug. To her relief it never budged. If it had swung open, she would've had to make a hasty retreat. She could feel emboldened as long as Toru-chan was beside her; otherwise, she was at least as shy and timid as the young master next door.

In her dreams, she would unlatch the wicket and exchange pleasantries with the young master. Sometimes he would come through to join her. Your cherry tree is putting on a fine display; Mother and I are enjoying it, too, he'd say. And she wouldn't hang back: Tell me, she'd say, where will you go to middle school next year? Are you going to try for a private school?

His eyes downcast, the young master answers: We can't afford a private school with my father gone. I don't know what's going to happen. The sister says: Our father's gone, too, but my mother wants to send me to private school. She says she's had enough of people's attitude at the school where

I go now, because of Toru-chan. And I know how she feels. The young master says: Wherever we may go to school, we'll still be neighbours, we can always meet like this. The sister smiles delightedly.

In reality, she turned twelve and started at a private girls' school without having so much as found out the young master next door's name. As her school was on the same line as her brother's, she set out with Toru-chan in the mornings and they boarded the heaving tram together. The English she now began to study intrigued Toru-chan, who would pore over a page of her textbook while drawing alphabet-like squiggles in his exercise book. He had his own homework, a diary to keep. He could write the basic hiragana script and simple kanji and do sums if they didn't involve double digits. However, as he lacked the worldly skills needed to reduce past events to neat stock phrases, the diary assignment weighed heavily on Toru-chan. He preferred to draw. His round face was becoming more angular, and his little sister's chest began to fill out.

Toru-chan's teacher sometimes visited on a Sunday and gave him a game of 'baseball'. Toru-chan took up the batter's stance and from six feet away the teacher pitched him a large, soft rubber ball. Even at that distance, it was hard for him to hit. Although his sister had her doubts – why this playacting when he had no idea what a game of baseball was like? – Toru-chan himself seemed to rejoice in these visits by the male teacher, and so did their mother. When Sensei and Toru-chan and their mother were in the garden, Louis the pointer, tail wagging madly in front of his kennel, would wheedle to join in.

The sister wasn't sure how much longer Toru-chan could remain at his present school. He clearly couldn't go there indefinitely, in any case. It was nothing more than a couple of special classes in borrowed rooms at a state primary school, but Toru-chan was satisfied, and their mother counted on the kind teacher who volunteered his time to visit them at home. Thinking of the future made the sister anxious. What would become of Toru-chan? But this concern rested on the assumption that Toru-chan would live as long as she did. After his death, she was made to realize that she had been taking that completely for granted.

The winter she turned thirteen, Toru-chan caught a cold which didn't improve for a month, and then he developed a high fever. At the hospital, he was found to have pneumonia, and the next day his heart stopped. His sister, arriving home from school as usual, noticed the change that had come over the house. In the kitchen, she could see her aunt, who lived far away and was almost a stranger. Their mother stayed seated at the head of the futon on which lay Toru-chan, and when she approached her brother, the aunt left off her bustling and joined them, weeping aloud. Whether their mother had cried then she couldn't remember clearly. She wasn't sure whether she had herself. She didn't think she'd cried, much. She'd barely even glanced at her mother's face, let alone been able to look at Toru-chan's. She was terrified by the suddenness of what had happened.

Toru-chan's funeral took place two days later, in the daytime. Quietly entering the garden by the front gate, his teachers and classmates approached the altar set up in the living room and offered incense. Her own teacher and class president attended, to her surprise. There were uncles and cousins on both her mother's and her father's side, along with other adults whose ties with her family she didn't know. And there, in the corner of the garden, stood the young master and his mother. The thrill it gave her to see they'd come made her instantly ashamed. Here Toru-chan was dead and she was her same old self. Still, she couldn't take her eyes off the pair from next door. Her heart pounded: what if the young master looked her way? He was in school uniform, his mother in black mourning. The sister had been wearing her school's sailor dress for three days now, she realized, hastily straightening the pleats.

The funeral was nearly over when the mother and son from next door burned incense. Having watched them do so and turn to leave, the sister hurried out of the living room and down the corridor. If she opened the bathroom window, she had a view of the front gate to the left and the low wicket to the right. Holding her breath, she stared out. The bathroom tiles were painfully cold against the soles of her feet. The neighbours came into view at once. They walked up to the wicket in the wall, the mother matter-of-factly pushed the little door open, and they disappeared through it without a word or backward glance. The sister drew a deep breath through her mouth. She'd been right. She'd had a feeling those two would use the wicket at a time like this. The next day, she went into the garden and gave it a push with the flat of her hand. Nothing had changed; it was still stuck tight.

The daughter who was once a little sister had believed that memory for a good thirty years. The mother and son next door had moved elsewhere twenty years ago, and the people who took their place had rebuilt. In the course of repairs to the garden wall, the wicket had been taken out and the opening filled in with cement blocks, and she hadn't given the doorway another thought. Except when she was reminded of Toru-chan's funeral; then, the image of the departing neighbours would come back to her. At the time, she had gone on dreaming of slipping next door and coming face to face with the boy of her own age, the young master. Hello, aren't the clouds beautiful in the sunset? one of them might say, and the other would reply, equally naturally, Hello, I have an English test tomorrow.

She knew these things belonged in dreams. Of course she'd never spoken to the young master or opened the wicket herself. But she didn't doubt that the neighbours had actually come through the wicket to pay their last respects at Toru-chan's funeral. Hadn't she turned pale as she'd watched the door open and their figures pass out of sight, because wasn't it at that very moment that the fact of Toru-chan's death was borne in on her, who had been his sister, and she'd had to admit it? Yet, as she passed through her forties and approached fifty, she was tempted when she saw her mother's aging face to question the very existence of that door. It struck her, moreover, that the neighbours would hardly have come directly into the garden by the back way on just that one occasion. Even supposing she hadn't imagined the door, first they'd have had to claw out a dozen rusty nails and rip off several boards.

She could think of no reason why they would go to all that trouble to come around by the back.

For a while, she had repeatedly dreamed of the two figures letting themselves into the garden, then returning the way they came. Sometimes the thirteen-year-old daughter would go through the wicket door and chat with the young master, who would have just stepped out into the garden. As he joined her there for a stroll, they would talk on and off about nothing in particular. These quiet, uneventful dreams continued. Always, somewhere in the background lay Toru-chan's body, gone cold.

At some point – it might have been within Louis's lifetime – her mother had passed on the news that a high wall had been built in the yard at Toru-chan's school. Somebody she'd known when Toru-chan was a pupil there had telephoned to tell her. Her mother and the other parents met to discuss what should be done, and the daughter who was once a little sister, after hesitating for several days, set out on her own for Toru-chan's old school. She was attending university by then and had a fairly free timetable.

Though the tram they used to take was no longer running, she could still picture the school clearly. She used to call in for Toru-chan on her way home, on days when she could leave her middle school early, as often happened on Saturdays. His school had consisted of two classrooms at a state primary, the two downstairs rooms nearest the gate. Though at fifteen Toru-chan was a middle-school pupil, his class was still housed in the primary school; she didn't know how this had come about. The teacher who used to come and play baseball had been in charge of the middle-school class. Their classroom had held eight desks in a circle, a blackboard with flowers and the sun and children's faces done in pink, yellow and blue chalk, and cheery designs taped to the window panes. The little sister had been envious of all that space with so few desks. There was a terrace outside, next to which were kept two rabbits and a tethered goat. She'd been told that the pupils took care of them together.

The sister felt dizzy as she neared Toru-chan's school. As she got within sight of the gate, her ears started to ring and her steps slowed. It was a weekday lunchtime and playing children thronged the yard. She looked in at the gate. Their cries at play swelled and surged across the schoolyard, more like the din of a large factory than human voices. There was no sign of the rabbits and the goat beside the terrace to the right of the gate, and the colourful decorations were gone from the windows of the classroom that had been Toru-chan's school. Since standing outside only made her more conspicuous, she went in, turning not right but left, along the concrete-walled perimeter. After fifteen feet or so she stopped short. A six-foot-high wall of corrugated iron jutted out from the concrete. It extended about fifteen feet into the yard.

Toru-chan, the rumour was right, they've built this horrid wall, she muttered under her breath as she walked beside the corrugated iron. There were no openings through which to enter nor windows to see inside. Stacked cement blocks were positioned to keep the sheet iron upright, and there were probably supporting posts on the other side. Though it was only a sheet-metal fence, it had clearly taken a serious construction job to build it from scratch. Children scudded around the sister as she walked its length. No one questioned what she was doing there.

The wall then made a right angle and ran another fifteen feet. This side, too, was featureless corrugated iron. What they'd done was wall off a square in the corner of the yard. Just before this second side abutted the concrete wall, there was a doorway in it, connected by a short corrugated-iron roof to the end of the building. Toru-chan's school must have been moved to that end. Did this mean that the special-class pupils, assigned the classrooms furthest from the gate, came and went to their desks via this passageway, and spent their breaks in the walled-off area? There was another door that opened into the yard where the roofed passage met the building.

What a squash, Toru-chan. She approached the entrance near the classrooms. It was fitted with a simple plywood door, fastened by a bar that could be raised and lowered. Once all the pupils arrived in the morning, was the passageway entrance locked from the outside until home time? Surely not, she frowned. She opened it, entered and peeked first of all into the nearest classroom. The circle of desks and the happy drawings on the blackboard were the same, but the windows were bare. This room would take about seven pupils, and she supposed the middle-school class used the next room. About fifteen children, in all. Were they outside right now, in the corrugated-iron enclosure? Toru-chan, too, would have had

49

to take the iron passageway to the iron yard. He wouldn't have understood why. He wouldn't understand, but he'd go quietly. Because the teachers said so. Because he loved the teachers and didn't want to make them sad.

If anyone had tried to explain that his school had screened off the area under pressure from the PTA of the primary school from which it borrowed the classrooms, on the grounds that letting the normal children be exposed to the daily sight of children like that might have educationally undesirable effects, it would have meant nothing to him. All the to-and-fro between the parents and the school over exactly how tall to make the wall, how big an area to secure and how to partition it off would also be irrelevant to Toru-chan. He couldn't know that the embarrassed school authorities had warned that the parents of those children would be up in arms themselves if the PTA went too far, to which the PTA had replied that that was as may be but their own children, being quick to imitate, made a show of dribbling and shambling and putting their hands down their trousers and playing with their willies.

Toru-chan couldn't care less about what people saw, or about trying to gauge their reactions. For that matter, Toru-chan has never called people names. The words don't exist in his mind. He doesn't attack people, either. On the other hand, he won't be moved an inch on something he doesn't want to do. If somebody he loves looks sad, Toru-chan dithers and tries to comfort them, but when *he* is sad he goes off and gives himself up to the feeling, without turning to other people for help.

Toru-chan follows the passageway to the partitioned-off section of the schoolyard. Even the sky is partitioned into a tight square. Toru-chan feels that much smaller, his own body pared down. At the back of the fenced part there is a flower bed. It was there all along, and since the wall went up it has fewer flowers, for lack of sun, while the ferns are thriving. Toru-chan applies his ear to the iron sheeting. He can hear the voices of the children playing on the other side. Sometimes the sound gathers itself like a wind and buffets the iron. Growing frustrated, Toru-chan places his hands against the metal. It is very cold and hard. He tries pushing. It is solidly anchored in the ground, and long metal posts support it every yard or two; the metal therefore only vibrates slightly and does not yield. Toru-chan presses his face against the wall and tries to see into the schoolyard. It's weird that he can't see it. The whole schoolyard was joined up, you could take in the one big area wherever you were. But no matter how wide he opens his short-sighted eyes, all he can see is the grey of the wall.

Toru-chan paces to the right along the corrugated iron. He encounters the concrete wall and turns back, heading left this time. He comes to the passageway, but turns back instead of going in. He does this again and again. Then he stands still inside the angle of the metal wall. What's happening? This thing has sprung up out of the ground, spoiling his fun, and it won't go away and it won't melt. The muffled voices of the children playing in the yard outside carry through the sheeting. Sometimes a bunch of voices knocks into him, and it hurts. Toru-chan hunkers down, afraid. The schoolyard he

51

knows has gone. He can't get to the schoolyard he knows. He can't get there from here, because this thing is in the way. His face twists sadly.

The steps that brought him to this point are likely to become a routine for Toru-chan over the days to come. The fear and the sadness will recur, too. Everything he's most scared of will start to crowd in, milling and roaring and whirling together just beyond the corrugated-iron wall – the swords and lances he knows from comic books, the rhino's horn and the tigers' and lions' fangs he saw at the zoo, and the things he sees on TV: the fire-breathing monster, bombs dropping from the sky, unseen guns bombarding a city, the creature from another planet, the volcano, the tornado that sucks everything up into the sky, the great waves of the sea, the thunder, the huge iceberg. He will crouch down in tears, trembling, moaning. If only his little sister was beside him, but even she has disappeared and is somewhere on the other side of the wall.

A black mongrel dog approaches him as he crouches there. It's Perry, the dog that belonged to his mother. Perry licks Toru-chan's left earlobe, and when Toru-chan lifts his face in surprise, he licks his tear-stained cheeks, then nuzzles and sniffs his shoulder, his arm. Toru-chan stops crying and places his hand on Perry's head. Perry dips his head as if in greeting, then sets off slowly towards the corrugated-iron wall. He walks right up to it. Noiselessly, without resistance, Perry's head sinks into the supposedly solid wall, his front paws are absorbed, his body vanishes and finally his tail, leaving a Perry-shaped hole in the corrugated iron.

A moment later, sensations begin wafting back through the hole to Toru-chan, who has been gaping, entranced, as Perry vanishes into the wall: a soft breeze, a scent of many roses, a bright cock-a-doodle-doo, a goat bleating to be fed, bunnies hopping and the playground full of children – his little sister among them – laughing, yelling, calling back and forth.

As he looks on agog, a single, distant bark sounds diffidently in his ears. Woof!

Toru-chan stands up unsteadily, pushes out his lips and tries it himself: Woof!

Then he starts telling his absent little sister about it: A dog came. Then there was a hole. Quick, come on through!

His little sister, now much older than himself, answers: Okay, but why don't *you* come on through, Toru-chan? If the hole's too small for you, I'll make it bigger. You never knew Perry, did you? Perry was our Mum's dog.

Toru-chan beams at the sound of her voice.

As for the actual corrugated-iron wall, a year – or perhaps it was two – after it was erected in the schoolyard, it was finally taken down, partly as a result of an article in the press.

The daughter, once a little sister, returned when she was nearly fifty to live with her mother and keep her company, and one day she asked her, 'What'd you do if another dog like Perry turned up out of nowhere? I'm guessing that's very unlikely, though?'

Her eyes half-closed in the light from the garden, her mother answered with a slight nod.